D1094782

AUG 2015

For Tess and Filip. – An
For my dear friend Anita. – Jenny

First published in Belgium and Holland by Clavis Uitgeverij, Hasselt – Amsterdam, 2013
Copyright © 2013, Clavis Uitgeverij

English translation from the Dutch by Clavis Publishing Inc. New York
Copyright © 2015 for the English language edition: Clavis Publishing Inc. New York

Visit us on the web at www.clavisbooks.com

You Make Me Happy written by An Swerts and illustrated by Jenny Bakker
Original title: *Zo blij met jou*
Translated from the Dutch by Clavis Publishing

ISBN 978-1-60537-204-4

This book was printed in April 2015 at Proost Industries NV,
Everdongenlaan 23, 2300 Turnhout, Belgium

First Edition
10 9 8 7 6 5 4 3 2 1

An Swerts & Jenny Bakker

You Make Me Happy

Clavis

NEW YORK

Sofia sits at her bedroom window.
The people on the street are hurrying home,
closing their jackets against the brisk wind.
But Sofia doesn't see them.
She gazes dreamily into space and
blows little clouds on the window
so she can draw in them.
"What lovely little hearts!"
Mom says as she walks into the room.
"Dinner's ready, come and eat."
"Actually I'm not really hungry," Sofia sighs.
Mommy gives her a searching look.
"You're not ill, are you?"
Sofia shrugs. Small furrows appear on her forehead.

The next morning the weather is beautiful.
Mom is out, so Grandma picks Sofia up.
Together they'll walk to Grandpa.
"Do you want a bag of cookies to eat on the way?"
Grandma asks Sofia. Sofia shakes her head.
Strange, Grandma thinks,
Sofia never says no to cookies.
"Grandma, is it possible to love someone too much?"
Sofia looks worried.
Grandma smiles. "What do you mean?"
"So much that you'll die," Sofia says.
Grandma looks puzzled.
"Well, maybe not *actually* die," Sofia says quickly.
"But so much that you feel like you can't breathe."

"And at the same time you feel happy and
light headed and a little like a feather
in the wind?" Grandma asks.
"Yes," Sofia sighs with relief.
Grandma knows exactly what she means.

"It *is* possible to love someone that much,"
Grandma says. "But it's rare."
"How rare?" Sofia asks.
Grandma thinks. "More rare than…the pagalo flower in the jungle."
The *pagalo* flower?
Sofia has never heard of it, but Grandma makes
it sound like a very special flower.

"Tell me," Grandma says. "Who do you like so much?"

"A boy in my class," Sofia says softly.

"And why do you like him so much?"

"He makes funny faces when the teacher is writing on the blackboard,"

Sofia says with a twinkle in her eyes.

And she shows Grandma.

Grandma shakes with laughter.

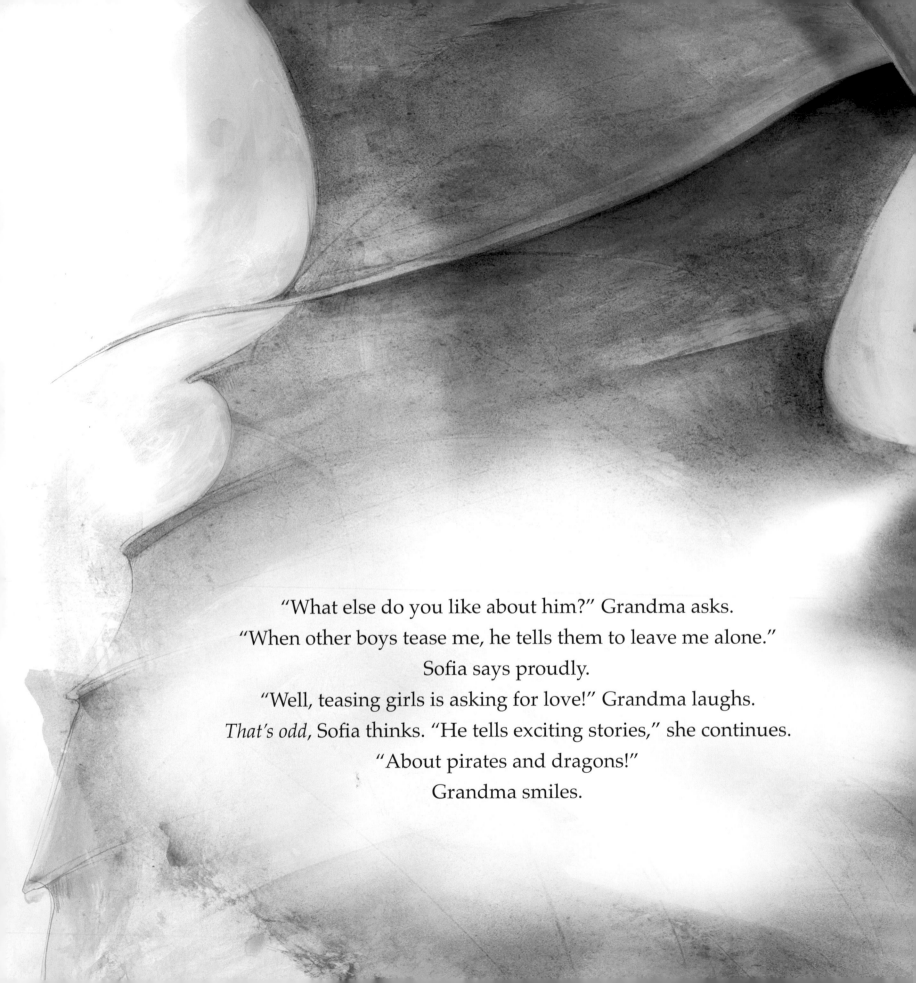

"What else do you like about him?" Grandma asks.
"When other boys tease me, he tells them to leave me alone."
Sofia says proudly.
"Well, teasing girls is asking for love!" Grandma laughs.
That's odd, Sofia thinks. "He tells exciting stories," she continues.
"About pirates and dragons!"
Grandma smiles.

"You have to tell him you like him," Grandma says firmly.
"Because when it's no longer a secret, you won't feel so anxious anymore.
Your heart might leap every now and then, but you'll be able to breathe better."
"Really?" Sofia can hardly believe it.
"Oh yes," Grandma nods. "You should tell him at your favorite spot!"

Grandma and Sofia have reached the lake. They are almost at Grandpa's now.
"Grandma, did you and Grandpa have a favorite spot?" Sofia asks curiously.
"Yes," Grandma says with sparkling eyes and she points to some boulders
between the reeds. "We went there to fold paper boats together. It was so very quiet
around us then. All you could hear was splashing water and quacking ducks."
"And that's where you told Grandpa?"
"Yes!" Grandma says. She looks like she's glowing.

"What exactly did you say?" Sofia asks.

"I told him that I liked him best of all the boys," Grandma says cheerfully.

"And I gave him a paper version of the boat of my dreams:

it was blue with white cabin windows."

Sofia stops in amazement. "Just like Grandpa's boat?" she asks, astonished.

Grandma nods.

"So…Grandpa's boat is the boat of your dreams!" Sofia exclaims.

"Oh, that's so sweet of him!"

"Who's so sweet?" Grandpa asks from the deck.
"You are!" Sofia calls out loudly.
"Because you built Grandma the boat of her dreams!"
She purses her lips and blows Grandpa a kiss.
Grandpa laughs and Storm wags his tail.

"Grandpa, did you give Grandma a gift too when she gave you her paper boat?"
"No," Grandpa says. Sofia looks disappointed. "But," Grandpa continues,
"when we were back at the lake the next day I gave her a ring."
"Oh!" Sofia cries delightedly. "With *real* diamonds?"
"No, little boys aren't that rich!" Grandpa laughs. "It was a ring from a vending
machine. But you know what *did* sparkle like real diamonds?"
Sofia really wants to know.
"Grandma's eyes!" says Grandpa happily.
"Silly Grandpa!" Sofia laughs. "But you *are* sweet."

"And what about you, Sofia?"
Grandma asks.
"How are you going to tell
that boy that you like him?"

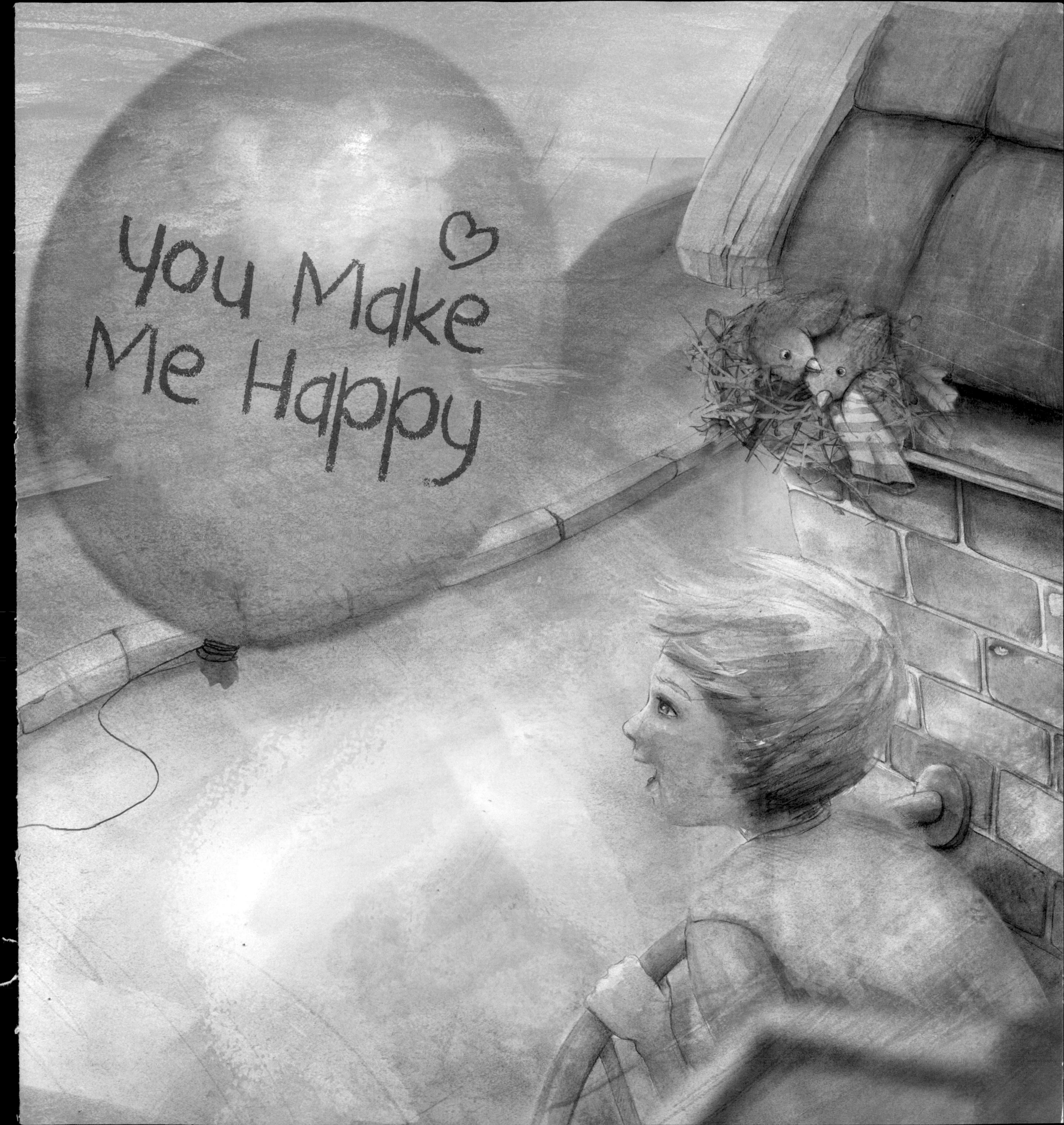
You Make
Me Happy